FAIR BALL!

14 GREAT STARS

FROM BASEBALL'S NEGRO LEAGUES

WRITTEN AND ILLUSTRATED BY

JONAH WINTER

FOR INDRA

Library of Congress Cataloging-in-Publication Data

Winter, Jonah

Fair ball!: 14 great stars from baseball's Negro league / by Jonah Winter: illustrated by the author. —1st ed.   p.   cm.

Summary: Short biographies of fourteen outstanding players in the United States Negro Leagues, including Pop Lloyd, Oscar Charleston, and Buck Leonard.

ISBN 0-590-39464-9

Baseball players—United States—Biography—Juvenile literature.

2. Afro-American baseball players—Biography—Juvenile literature.

3. Negro leagues—Juvenile literature. [1. Baseball players.

2. Afro-Americans—Biography. 3. Negro leagues.]

GV865.A1W56   1999

796.357'092'273—dc21   98-7603 CIP AC

10 9 8 7 6 5 4 3 2 1   9/9 0/0 01 02 03

Printed in Singapore   46

First edition, April 1999

The text type was set in Cooper Oldstyle Light.

Book design by David Caplan

INTRODUCTION

◆ ◆ ◆

EVERYONE has heard of Babe Ruth, Lou Gehrig, and Ty Cobb — three of baseball's all-time legends. But how many people have heard of Pop Lloyd, Oscar Charleston, or Buck Leonard? They were superstars of the Negro Leagues. The Negro Leagues were a strange chapter in American history. For almost sixty years, black men were not allowed to play in the major leagues. So they formed their own leagues. Just like the majors, these leagues had world series, all-star games, and legendary heroes.

Sometimes, Negro League teams would play major league teams in exhibition games. The major league white teams lost so often, they finally refused to play the black teams anymore. The truth is, many of the black stars from this era were just plain better than their white counterparts. Josh Gibson hit more home runs than Babe Ruth. Cool Papa Bell was faster than Ty Cobb. And Satchel Paige won more games than Cy Young.

There is a whole secret world of baseball legends from this time. It's time that everyone knew about at least a few of them.

RUBE FOSTER

NAME: Andrew "Rube" Foster
CAREER: 1902 – 26
TEAMS: Chicago American Giants
POSITIONS: Pitcher, manager, owner, commissioner

HEIGHT: 6'2"
WEIGHT: 200 – 300 pounds
BORN: September 17, 1879, Calvert, TX
DIED: December 9, 1930, Kankakee, IL

RUBE FOSTER was a HUGE man — he weighed three hundred pounds! And he was a great man. He did so many great things, it's hard to count them. Here are a few:

- He organized black baseball into the Negro National League.
- He was the greatest manager of all time.
- He was the best pitcher of his era, black or white.

As a pitcher, Rube once won 54 games in one season, losing only one! As a manager, he once led his team to 126 victories and 6 losses. His team was the Chicago American Giants, the winningest team in baseball history.

Manager Rube invented a whole new style of playing baseball. It was centered around bunting, stealing bases, and running fast all the time. He invented the hit-and-run play, the bunt-and-run play, the squeeze play, the double steal, and even the triple steal! He actually *fined* his players for not stealing bases!

Rube Foster made people proud to play in the Negro Leagues. That's one reason he's called "The Father of Black Baseball." If anyone ever deserved to be in the Baseball Hall of Fame, it's Rube Foster. And he is!

RUBE FOSTER

NAME: William Hendrick "Willie" Foster
CAREER: 1923 – 38
TEAMS: Memphis Red Sox, Chicago American Giants
POSITION: Pitcher

HEIGHT: 6´1˝
WEIGHT: 195 pounds
BORN: June 12, 1904, Calvert, TX
DIED: September 16, 1978, Lorman, MI

WILLIE FOSTER was the best left-handed pitcher in black baseball history. Being Rube Foster's younger half-brother, he had a lot to live up to. When Willie first started out, Rube tried to forbid him to play baseball. It didn't work. Willie joined the Memphis Red Sox. When Rube heard about this, he ordered the Red Sox manager to trade Willie to the Chicago American Giants, where he could manage his rookie half-brother.

This made Willie pretty mad. So he refused to follow any of Rube's orders. You see, Willie thought that that kind of thing would get him traded. Game after game, Willie lost — on purpose. But no matter how badly Willie played, Rube would not trade him.

Then one day Rube left the American Giants, and guess what? Willie took all of Rube's advice he had pretended not to hear and he used it to become the best lefty of his time, maybe of all time.

Willie threw all kinds of pitches — a fastball, a slider, a curveball, a breaking ball, and a very good change-up, to name a few. He kept batters guessing. Willie Foster was a wizard.

Here's the thing Willie was best at as a pitcher: control.

Willie Foster is in the Baseball Hall of Fame.

WILLIE FOSTER

SATCHEL PAIGE

NAME: Robert LeRoy "Satchel" Paige

CAREER: 1926 – 50

TEAMS: Pittsburgh Crawfords, Kansas City Monarchs

POSITION: Pitcher

HEIGHT: 6´4˝

WEIGHT: 180 pounds

BORN: July 7, 1906, Mobile, AL

DIED: June 8, 1982, Kansas City, MO

SATCHEL PAIGE was one of the best pitchers who ever lived. Some people say he was *the* best. He always put on a show for the crowds. He said funny things to the batters. He would say, "I'm not going to throw a yoke at your choke. I'm going to throw a pea at your knee." He had names for his pitches: Bee Ball, Jump Ball, Trouble Ball, and The Midnight Rider.

Then there was his famous Windmill Pitch. He wound up his arm several times, leaned way back, kicked his foot high in the air, then waited just a moment. When he finally threw the ball, it went so fast, people often couldn't see it. Catchers couldn't catch it. It hurt to catch his fastball.

Here are a few of Paige's "Rules for a Long, Healthy Life":

- ◆ Don't run.
- ◆ Eat boiled chicken.
- ◆ Jangle softly as you walk.

Satchel Paige pitched until he was fifty-nine years old — by far the oldest of any baseball player. (He ended his career in the majors.) No one is quite sure how many people he struck out, or how many games he completed. He probably completed around 2,600 games — almost 2,000 more than the official world champion, Cy Young.

Satchel Paige is in the Baseball Hall of Fame.

SATCHEL PAIGE

JOSH GIBSON

NAME: Joshua "Josh" Gibson

CAREER: 1929 – 46

TEAMS: Homestead Grays, Pittsburgh Crawfords

POSITION: Catcher

HEIGHT: 6'1"

WEIGHT: 210 pounds

BORN: December 21, 1911, Buena Vista, GA

DIED: January 20, 1947, Pittsburgh, PA

JOSH GIBSON was the greatest power-hitter who ever lived — better than Babe Ruth, better than Hank Aaron. Most record-books show him ending his career with 962 home runs. That's 200 more than the official record!

One year he hit 75 home runs. That's 14 more than the official record. One time, he hit a home run out of Yankee Stadium — over the fence, out onto the street. No one else in history has done that.

Gibson also got a lot of hits. His lifetime batting average was .354. Several seasons he hit over .400.

And guess what — he was also a nice guy! Men who played with him said he was just like a big kid, always eager to play the game. Had he not died young, at the age of thirty-six, there's no telling how many homers he could have hit.

Josh Gibson is in the Baseball Hall of Fame.

JOSH GIBSON

BIZ MACKEY

NAME: Raleigh "Biz" Mackey
CAREER: 1920 – 47
TEAMS: Hilldale Daisies, Baltimore
Elite Giants, Newark Eagles
POSITION: Catcher

HEIGHT: 6'0"
WEIGHT: 200 pounds
BORN: July 27, 1897, Eagle Pass, TX
DIED: (date unknown) 1959,
Los Angeles, CA

BIZ MACKEY may have been the best catcher of all time. He could throw out a base stealer without even standing up. That's because he had one of the fastest throwing arms of any catcher, living or dead. He could throw the ball straight at the second baseman's glove. Pitchers liked him because he could make a ball look like a strike by moving his glove into the strike zone really fast.

Now here's the amazing part: he could also hit! Here are his batting averages for nine seasons in a row: .423, .337, .350, .327, .315, .327, .337, .400, and .376. He could hit home runs, too. He was the first man to hit a homer in the brand-new baseball stadium in Tokyo, Japan.

In addition to all these things, he was a good role model for younger players. Biz Mackey didn't drink or smoke. He played until he was fifty years old. His lifetime batting average was .335.

BIZ MACKEY

BUCK LEONARD

NAME: Walter Fenner "Buck" Leonard

CAREER: 1933 – 50

TEAM: Homestead Grays

POSITION: First baseman

HEIGHT: 5´10˝

WEIGHT: 185 pounds

BORN: September 8, 1907, Rocky Mount, NC

DIED: November 27, 1997, Rocky Mount, NC

WHEN THE OLD-TIMERS sit around and discuss who the best first baseman of all time was — and this is all the old-timers do — it's a toss-up. The old white players and fans say Lou Gehrig. The old black players and fans say Buck Leonard.

The truth is, the two men were alike in a lot of ways. They were both powerful hitters who rarely missed a game. They both hit well under pressure. They were both gentlemen on and off the field. And they were both in the shadows of even more powerful hitters. For Lou Gehrig, it was Babe Ruth. For Buck Leonard, it was Josh Gibson.

The truth is, Buck Leonard didn't mind being in Josh Gibson's shadow. He didn't want the spotlight. He didn't need it. Leonard's lifetime batting average was .341. Gehrig's lifetime average was .340. The year before Willie Mays was getting his start in baseball, in 1947, Buck Leonard batted .410 for the season. He was forty years old — over the hill for a baseball player.

If only baseball fans of *all* colors could have seen Buck play — those acrobatic catches he made at first base, those screeching line-drive home runs he hit. The old-timers still talk about them.

Buck Leonard is in the Baseball Hall of Fame.

BUCK LEONARD

MULE SUTTLES

NAME: George "Mule" Suttles

CAREER: 1918 – 44

TEAMS: St. Louis Stars, Newark Eagles

POSITION: First baseman

HEIGHT: 6´3˝

WEIGHT: 215 pounds

BORN: March 2, 1901, Brockton, LA

DIED: (date unknown) 1968, Newark, NJ

MULE SUTTLES was a big, heavy, powerful hitter. He often led his league in home runs. Once he hit the ball 500 feet long and 60 feet high! Another time he hit the ball 600 feet! That may be the longest ball anyone has ever hit.

Mule Suttles was too big to be of much use on the field. He couldn't run very fast. But when he came up to bat, people would yell, "Kick, Mule! Kick, Mule!" He once said, "Don't worry about the Mule going blind, just load the wagon and give me the lines."

His lifetime batting average was .338.

MULE SUTTLES

BINGO DeMOSS

NAME: Elwood "Bingo" DeMoss
CAREER: 1910 – 30; 1942 – 45
TEAMS: Indianapolis ABCs, Chicago
American Giants, Detroit Stars
POSITIONS: Second baseman, manager

HEIGHT: 6'2"
WEIGHT: 175 pounds
BORN: September 5, 1889, Topeka, KA
DIED: January 26, 1965, Chicago, IL

BINGO DeMOSS was the greatest second baseman in black baseball history. He was a fast and accurate thrower and he always got a good jump on the ball. No one was better at turning the double play. He could whip the ball to first base in midair without even looking. At bat, Bingo was also a whiz, though not at all a power-hitter. His specialty was bunting. He could "bunt on a dime," as the old folks say.

Bingo probably had the best control of any hitter in his league. He could put the ball anywhere he wanted to. Often he would make sacrifice hits just to advance the runner. You see, for Bingo, the team always came first. So, even though he was one of the game's greatest hitters, he made a lot of outs. That's why some of his batting averages were only in the mid 200s.

Bingo DeMoss was a baseball player's baseball player and a classic athlete.

Plus, he always played second base with a toothpick in his mouth.

BINGO DeMOSS

MARTIN DIHIGO

NAME: Martin "El Maestro" Dihigo
CAREER: 1923 – 45
TEAMS: Cuban Stars, Hilldale Daisies, New York Cubans
POSITIONS: Second baseman, outfielder, pitcher, first baseman, third baseman, shortstop, catcher, manager

HEIGHT: 6′3″
WEIGHT: 190 pounds
BORN: May 25, 1905, Matanzas, Cuba
DIED: May 22, 1971, Cienfuegos, Cuba

MARTIN DIHIGO could do everything — pitch, hit, play all the positions, and even manage. He started out as a second baseman but soon was able to play EVERY position — in one game, sometimes! He often led the league in both batting and pitching. One season, he posted a 0.90 earned run average and a .387 batting average. Another season, he hit the ball 500 feet! This is how he earned his Spanish nickname, "El Maestro," which in English means "the Master."

Martin Dihigo was from Cuba, and he's probably the all-time greatest baseball player to come from Latin America — and there have been quite a few. Baseball has always been popular there. Many players, both black and white, used to play in Cuba and Mexico during the winter. Many Cubans also came to America to play baseball. Most of them, like Dihigo, were too dark-skinned to play in the majors.

Martin Dihigo is the only player in history to be elected to the Baseball Hall of Fame in four countries: the United States, Cuba, Mexico, and Venezuela.

MARTIN DIHIGO

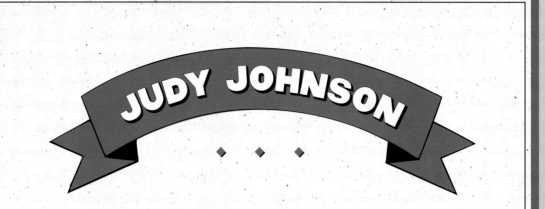

JUDY JOHNSON

NAME: William Julius "Judy" Johnson
CAREER: 1918 – 37
TEAMS: Hilldale Daisies,
Pittsburgh Crawfords
POSITION: Third baseman

HEIGHT: 5´11˝
WEIGHT: 150 pounds
BORN: October 26, 1900, Snow Hill, MD
DIED: June 15, 1989, Wilmington, DE

JUDY JOHNSON was a man. He was nicknamed Judy because he reminded some guy of this other guy named Judy. Who knows why the first guy was called Judy? It's probably not important. What is important is that Judy Johnson was one of the smartest baseball players ever.

With a lifetime batting average of .301, Judy Johnson was not the most powerful hitter. He wasn't the fastest runner. But he made up for this by outthinking his opponents. He was a wizard at stealing the other team's signals. At bat, he often puffed out his left sleeve so he could get dusted by a pitch and sent to first base. And he was known for roughing up the ball with sandpaper when the other team wasn't looking.

But Judy was best known for his fielding. Defensively, no other third baseman in history could touch Judy Johnson, the old-timers claim. He timed his leaps perfectly and had deadly aim with his throwing arm. And he was a really, really nice guy whom everyone liked.

Judy Johnson is in the Baseball Hall of Fame.

JUDY JOHNSON

BOOJUM WILSON

NAME: Ernest Judson "Boojum" Wilson
CAREER: 1922 – 45
TEAMS: Baltimore Black Sox, Homestead Grays, Philadelphia Stars
POSITIONS: Third baseman, first baseman

HEIGHT: 5'8"
WEIGHT: 185 pounds
BORN: February 28, 1899, Remington, VA
DIED: June 26, 1963, Washington, D.C.

BOOJUM WILSON may have been the scariest baseball player who ever lived. He was built like a superhero, with a huge upper body and a tiny little waist, and he loved to get in fights. But there were not too many men brave enough to tangle with Boojum. One time a base runner slid into Boojum with his spikes flying. Boojum swatted him aside like a fly and then picked him up and threw him 20 feet!

At the plate, there was no hitter more feared than Boojum Wilson. Against major-league pitchers, he hit .442. His lifetime batting average was .370, third best in Negro League history. But that only tells half the story. He would always watch the first two pitches to see what kind of stuff the pitcher had. And he would ALWAYS swing at the third pitch, no matter where it was. Once a pitcher threw Boojum a ball so low, it bounced in the dirt way in front of home plate. Boojum bent down and hit that thing out of the park! He could hit any kind of pitch.

He got his nickname from the sound his line drives made as they bounced off the distant fences: BOOJUM! Satchel Paige claimed Boojum was the only man who knew how to hit his pitches.

BOOJUM WILSON

POP LLOYD

NAME: John Henry "Pop" Lloyd
CAREER: 1906 – 32
TEAMS: Philadelphia Giants, New York Lincoln Giants, Chicago American Giants, Brooklyn Royal Giants, Atlantic City Bacharach Giants
POSITION: Shortstop

HEIGHT: 5'11"
WEIGHT: 180 pounds
BORN: April 25, 1884, Palatka, FL
DIED: March 19, 1965, Atlantic City, NJ

POP LLOYD was the greatest shortstop ever. Even people who also saw his white rival for that spot, Honus Wagner, say Pop Lloyd was the best. He played shortstop with unequaled beauty and grace. He had long arms and used to dig balls out of the dirt like a shovel. When he played in Cuba, they called him "El Cuchara," or "the Spoon."

He was a classic, natural ballplayer. One day in 1910, he got a chance to prove himself against Ty Cobb, thought to be the greatest white ballplayer ever.

Ty Cobb held the all-time major league records for hits, stolen bases, and batting average. He also hated black people. (Ty Cobb hated people in general.) In an exhibition game against Lloyd's black team, Ty Cobb decided he was going to embarrass this guy Lloyd everyone was talking about — and steal a base. Lloyd knew that Ty Cobb was famous for twisting his spikes into the shortstop as he came flying through the air.

Lloyd was ready for him, wearing his cast-iron shin guards. When Cobb tried to twist his spikes into Lloyd's leg, Lloyd hooked Cobb's spikes on his shin guard and threw the feisty base stealer into center field. Spitting and cursing, Ty Cobb stormed back to the dugout.

Cobb didn't try to steal any more bases off Lloyd. In fact, Ty Cobb never played a black team again after that day.

Pop Lloyd is in the Baseball Hall of Fame. His lifetime batting average was .339.

POP LLOYD

COOL PAPA BELL

NAME: James Thomas "Cool Papa" Bell
CAREER: 1922 – 46
TEAMS: St. Louis Stars, Homestead Grays, Pittsburgh Crawfords
POSITION: Center fielder

HEIGHT: 5´11˝
WEIGHT: 150 pounds
BORN: May 17, 1903, Starkville, MI
DIED: March 7, 1991, St. Louis, MO

COOL PAPA BELL was the fastest baseball player ever. During his baseball career, he was the fastest man alive. Even the Olympic running champion Jesse Owens refused to race him because he knew Bell was the fastest. Cool Papa Bell ran so fast, he could often steal two bases instead of just one.

According to his roommate, Satchel Paige, Cool Papa Bell was so fast, he could turn off the light and be in bed before it was dark. As a joke, Bell once rigged the light switch in their hotel room so that the light stayed on a few seconds after you turned it off. When Paige came back, Bell turned off the light switch and jumped into bed before it was dark. They had a laugh over that!

One year, Bell stole 175 bases — by far the world record. Once he scored from first base on a bunt. Once he hit a ball up the middle — then supposedly ran so fast, he was hit by his own ball and called out. His lifetime batting average was .341.

Cool Papa Bell was a fast fielder, too. He could run down an infield pop fly from the outfield and pick it out of the air with one hand.

Cool Papa Bell is in the Baseball Hall of Fame.

COOL PAPA BELL

OSCAR CHARLESTON

NAME: Oscar McKinley Charleston
CAREER: 1915 – 54
TEAMS: Indianapolis ABCs, Harrisburg Giants, Homestead Grays, Pittsburgh Crawfords, Philadelphia Stars, Indianapolis Clowns
POSITIONS: Center fielder, first baseman, manager

HEIGHT: 6'0"
WEIGHT: 190 pounds
BORN: October 14, 1896, Indianapolis, IN
DIED: October 6, 1954, Philadelphia, PA

WHO IS THE GREATEST baseball player of all time? The famous major-league manager John McGraw said it was Oscar Charleston. A lot of other people said so, too. Charleston played center field with the speed and grace of Wille Mays and Joe DiMaggio. He hit and stole bases like Ty Cobb. And his home runs reminded people of Babe Ruth and Josh Gibson.

Oscar Charleston was built like Babe Ruth, but he was a much meaner ballplayer. Like Boojum Wilson, he liked to fight. Like Ty Cobb, he had a horrible temper. He was scared of nobody. He had steel-gray eyes that looked right through people. He had ice water running through his veins, or so they say.

How great a player was he? There were five seasons in which Charleston hit over .400. His lifetime average is .357. One time he hit a ball so hard, it made the pitcher start to cry. In the field, he caught fly balls with his back to them. It was like he had eyes in the back of his head. Sometimes, to please the crowd, he'd do a somersault before he caught the ball.

Oscar Charleston is in the Baseball Hall of Fame. Maybe someday, every baseball fan will know his name.

OSCAR CHARLESTON

NO BOOK CAN CORRECT the injustice of segregated baseball. All of the players in this book, except for Satchel Paige, were underpaid and largely ignored during their careers. No baseball cards were made of them. When their playing days were over, many of them took up jobs as mailmen, bartenders, and janitors. Aside from being elected to the Baseball Hall of Fame years later, as most of the players in this book were, they were all but swept under the rug of official baseball history.

The good news is: With every passing year, there are more books about these amazing athletes. Finally, a larger number of people are learning about their greatness.

Sadly, though, none of the players in this book are still alive to hear all the chatter. But if there's baseball in Heaven, as well there should be, maybe Satchel Paige and Babe Ruth are both on the same all-star team — a team that would make the 1927 Yankees look like Little League material. . . .

MY ULTIMATE
ALL-STAR TEAMS IN THE SKY

AMERICAN LEAGUE	NATIONAL LEAGUE
Manager: Rube Foster	**Manager:** John McGraw
Pitcher: Satchel Paige	**Pitcher:** Christy Mathewson
Catcher: Josh Gibson	**Catcher:** Biz Mackey
1st Baseman: Lou Gehrig	**1st Baseman:** Buck Leonard
2nd Baseman: Bingo DeMoss	**2nd Baseman:** Rogers Hornsby
3rd Baseman: Jimmie Foxx	**3rd Baseman:** Boojum Wilson
Shortstop: Pop Lloyd	**Shortstop:** Honus Wagner
Left Fielder: Ted Williams	**Left Fielder:** Oscar Charleston
Center Fielder: Joe DiMaggio	**Center Fielder:** Cool-Papa Bell
Right Fielder: Babe Ruth	**Right Fielder:** Martin Dihigo